MAGIC SHOELACES

written and illustrated by
Audrey Wood

Published by Child's Play (International) Ltd

© 1980 M. Twinn.   ISBN 0–85953–321–2 (soft cover)   Printed in India
Millennium edition 1999.   ISBN 0–85953–109–0 (hard cover)
                        Library of Congress Number 90–49097
             A catalogue reference for this book is available from the British Library.

Matthew! Mother said you are going to be late
for play-school! My friends are coming over, and
I need to mop this floor. How many times do I have
to tell you: hurry up and tie those shoes!

I just did, Jessica!
They keep coming untied!

Well, tie them again! Mother always says,
"Practice makes perfect".

Right over left, left over right, make a loop, circle the loop under the bridge, pull. There, that should do it!

Good-bye, sister. See you later.

Oh, Nooooo! My shoelaces did it again.

Remember what
Mother says . . .
"Those who do not
keep their laces tied
will fall down."

These shoelaces are nothing but trouble.

Hey guys! Take a look at that kid's laces.

Oh, no!
Not again!

What are those worms doing crawling out of your shoes? Can't keep your laces tied! Ha! ha! ha!

I'm sick and tired of lacing and tying. I don't need shoelaces. I'll just take them out!

Ahhhh!
That's better!

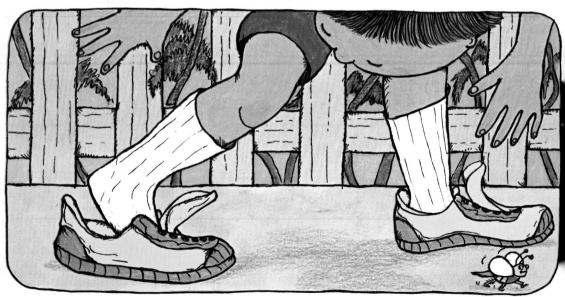

Now what's happening?

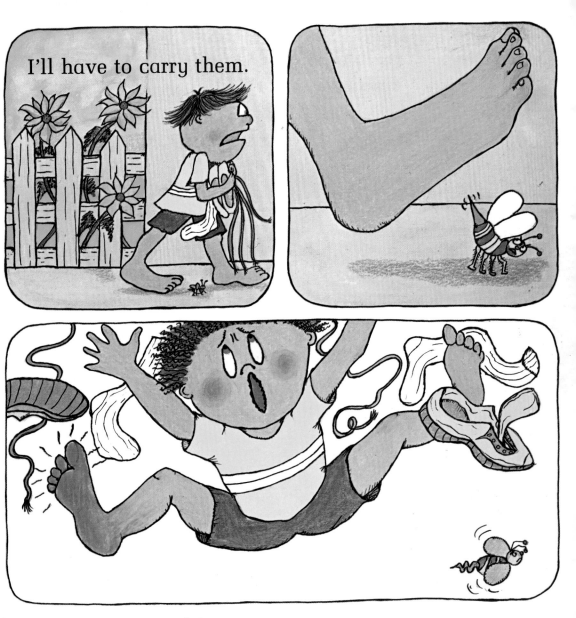

Ooooooooooouch!

My poor foot! Why do shoelaces have to be so much trouble?

I wish . . .

I wish . . .

I wish shoelaces would not always come untied.

Magic shoelaces! Step right up! Magic shoelaces!
No more "Practice makes perfect". Guaranteed
not to come untied!

You can't buy them,
only swap.
Mine for yours,
Now, hop, hop, hop!

Go ahead and choose,
red, yellow, or blue.
Satisfaction guaranteed.

In and out, tie them tight: magic laces stay on right!

These laces really are magic! I have walked all the way to play-school and they haven't come undone!

Today, children,
we will learn to swim.
But first, you must
take off your shoes
and put them
in the boxes.

I . . . can't . . . get . . .

. . these magic
shoelaces untied.
They won't come off!

Whew! Am I hot!
The pool looks so good
and cool. I just have to . .
I've got to . . .

GO-O-O-O-O-O SWIMMING!

Young man, get out this instant!
Shoes are not allowed in the pool!

No more swimming for you today.   Go straight home.

Squash, squish . . .

squush, flump, splosh . . .

splosh, squash . . .

splush, squish . . .

Jessica, I'm home.

For heaven's sake! How dare you walk on my nice clean floor with all that mud! Go out and take those shoes off, and don't come back in here until you do.

My shoelaces won't come untied!

That's the most ridiculous thing I've ever heard. Laces *always* come untied.

These aren't just any old laces. I got them from a magic man. They are magic.

Look! Scissors won't cut them . . .

Rocks won't smash them . . .

These laces won't break.

I've always wanted
magic laces . . .

I bet Matthew knows a
magic way to get them off.
He just doesn't want to.

Matthew, dear! If you get
those laces undone,
I will buy them from you.

And I'll even throw in
my nice, white shoelaces.
What a bargain!

She just doesn't understand.

The magic man said, you cannot buy them . . .

only . . .

SWAP!

Boy, what a dumb deal you made, Matthew.
My ugly old laces for your magic ones.

These shoelaces may not be
magic, Jessica . . .

But with practice . . .

they'll be perfect!